Henry and the Hand-Me-Downs

Text Copyright © Evans Brothers Ltd. 2005. Illustration Copyright
© Evans Brothers Ltd. 2005. First published by Evans Brothers
Limited, 2A Portman Mansions, Chiltern Street, London W1U 6NR,
United Kingdom. This edition published under license from Zero to
Ten Limited. All rights reserved. Printed in China. This edition
published in 2005 by Gingham Dog Press, an imprint of School
Specialty Publishing, a member of the School Specialty Family.

Library of Congress-in-Publication Data is on file with the publisher.

Send all inquiries to:
School Specialty Publishing
8720 Orion Place
Columbus, OH 43240-2111

ISBN 0-7696-4209-8

1 2 3 4 5 6 7 8 9 10 EVN 10 09 08 07 06 05

Henry and the Hand-Me-Downs

By Jillian Powell

Illustrated by Belinda Worsley

GINGHAM DOG
PRESS

Columbus, Ohio

Henry was the baby
of his family.

This was fun.

But it was not always fair.
Henry never got anything new.

He got Ben's old computer.

He got Tom's old bike.

He got Josh's old bed.

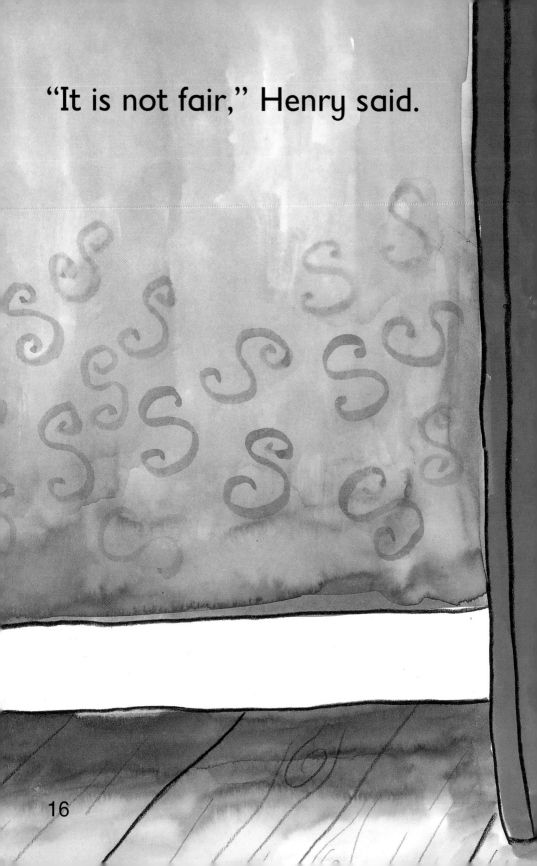

"It is not fair," Henry said.

He went to find
something that was
just his.

He found a feather.

But it was a bird's feather.

He found a shell.

But it was a snail's shell.

He found a ball.

But it was a dog's ball.

Henry was sad.
He did not find anything
that was just his.

25

Then, he saw something.

He stood on his head.
He did a flip.

Henry found something that was just his—his shadow!

Words I Know

always	new
found	old
got	saw
just	was

Think About It!

1. What things did Henry get from his older brothers?
2. What did Henry find on his hunt?
3. Who owned the things Henry found?
4. What did Henry find at the end of the story that was just his?

The Story and You

1. Have you ever gotten hand-me-downs from your older brothers or sisters? Did you like them?
2. Henry's shadow was special. It was just his. What makes you special?